This Little Tiger book belongs to:

_____

_____

_____

For Honor Rose
~ A M

Sometimes it's the smallest of things that make the biggest impact
~ C P

LITTLE TIGER PRESS LTD,
1 Coda Studios,
189 Munster Road, London SW6 6AW
Imported into the EEA by Penguin Random House Ireland,
Morrison Chambers, 32 Nassau Street, Dublin D02 YH68
www.littletiger.co.uk

First published in Great Britain 2015
This edition published 2016
Text copyright © Angela McAllister 2015
Illustrations copyright © Caroline Pedler 2015

Angela McAllister and Caroline Pedler have asserted
their rights to be identified as the author and illustrator of this
work under the Copyright, Designs and Patents Act, 1988
A CIP catalogue record for this book is available from the British Library

A Mouse So Small

Angela McAllister

Caroline Pedler

LiTTLE TiGER
LONDON

A cold wind rustled through the wood.

"Autumn is nearly over," Bear told Millie Mouse.
"It's time for my long winter sleep."

Millie gave Bear a hug. His tummy rumbled.

"Are you hungry?" she asked.

"Yes," yawned Bear, "but I can't stop to eat –
I might fall asleep, right here in the wood!"

"You must hurry home, Bear!"
exclaimed Millie. "Goodbye!"
"See you in the spring,"
he promised.

"Poor Bear is going to bed hungry," thought Millie as her friend tramped away through the autumn leaves. "I have to help him!"

She looked around.

"Ooh, blackberries! Bear would love those," she thought.

But the blackberries were too
high to pick. Millie frowned.
   "I'll get you somehow," she said.
"I won't let Bear go hungry."

Millie tried jumping, but
her legs were too short.

She tried knocking them
down with a stick, but still
she couldn't reach.

Then she spotted a tree stump.
Up she scrambled.

"Just a bit higher," Millie
puffed as she stretched towards
the blackberries . . .

But as she grabbed a branch to pull the berries close, she wibbled and wobbled and slipped off the stump!

"Help!" yelled Millie, dangling from the blackberry bush.

Luckily, Fox was passing by.
 "You're too small to climb
up there," he said, lifting
her down.
 "I'm not too small,"
huffed Millie. "This blackberry
bush is too tall!"

"Let me help," Fox smiled
as he pulled the branch close.
      Millie picked the three fattest
blackberries.
      "Thank you," she said.
"These are for Bear."

Millie set off through the wood to Bear's den.

But three fat blackberries were heavy to carry.

First she dropped one. Then another.

"You're very greedy for such a small mouse," chuckled Squirrel.

"I'm not a small mouse!" insisted Millie. "I haven't finished growing yet. And I'm not greedy either – these berries are for Bear."

"Why don't you pull them along on a leaf?" suggested Squirrel.

Millie found a big leaf and piled the blackberries on top.

"Thank you, Squirrel," she said.

But Squirrel had already hurried away to bury food for the winter.

Millie pulled the berries up the hill.

"I hope Bear is still awake," she puffed.

Suddenly she heard a grumbling voice.

"What a nuisance! How annoying!"
Hedgehog had something stuck
in his prickles.

"It's a nut!" said Millie.
"It's in a very awkward
place," muttered Hedgehog.
"I can help," cried Millie.
She stood on tiptoes and
reached carefully into his
prickles. "Got it!" she cheered.
"You can have it!" grunted
Hedgehog and he scurried off.

Millie added the nut to her pile.
But when she tugged the leaf,
everything toppled off and
rolled away down
the hill!

One berry fell into a rabbit hole.
One rolled under a hedge.
And Hedgehog's nut plopped into a puddle!
"Come back!" cried Millie as she raced after them.

When she reached the bottom of the hill there was just one berry left!

"I can't even run as fast as a blackberry!" she huffed. "I'm just too *small*!"

Millie sat and sighed sadly.
A flock of birds flew overhead,
on their way to find a warmer home.
A chilly breeze rustled the leaves
and rattled the fir cones.
"Winter's nearly here," thought Millie,
"and Bear is going to bed hungry."

She picked up the last berry.
"At least this will be better
than nothing," she decided,
and she started back up
the hill.

When Millie arrived at Bear's den he was
very surprised to see her.

"I didn't want you to be hungry," explained Millie,
offering Bear the blackberry. "I wanted to bring
you lots, but I was too small to reach them,
and too small to carry them, and too
small to catch them when they
rolled away!"

Bear lifted her gently onto his paw.

"You may be small, Millie," he said
with a smile, "but you have a
very BIG heart!"

He pointed inside his store cupboard
and Millie stared in amazement.
It was full of food that Bear
had gathered!

"Berries grow on bushes and nuts grow on trees,"
said Bear, "but best friends aren't so easy to find."
   Millie gave Bear her BIGGEST hug. And together,
the two friends sat and watched the sun sink
in the autumn sky, until it was time for a
long winter sleep.